along towards a clump of tall, ragged furze-bushes. He knew of a
sheltered place in the middle of the clump – almost like a little
cave. It would be warmer there, and he might find a tuft of grass
that was not frosted, to eat when morning came.

That Christmas Eve the donkey was feeling very lonely. Even the brown cow that lived on the common had been taken back to her shed. The donkey had heard the old woman who came to fetch her say, "Come along, Brownie, come along, my dear. There's some warm straw and some beautiful hay for a treat, because tomorrow is Christmas Day."

The donkey had heard of Christmas. He did not know much about it, but if it was anything to do with hay, he was sure it must be comfortable.

 4

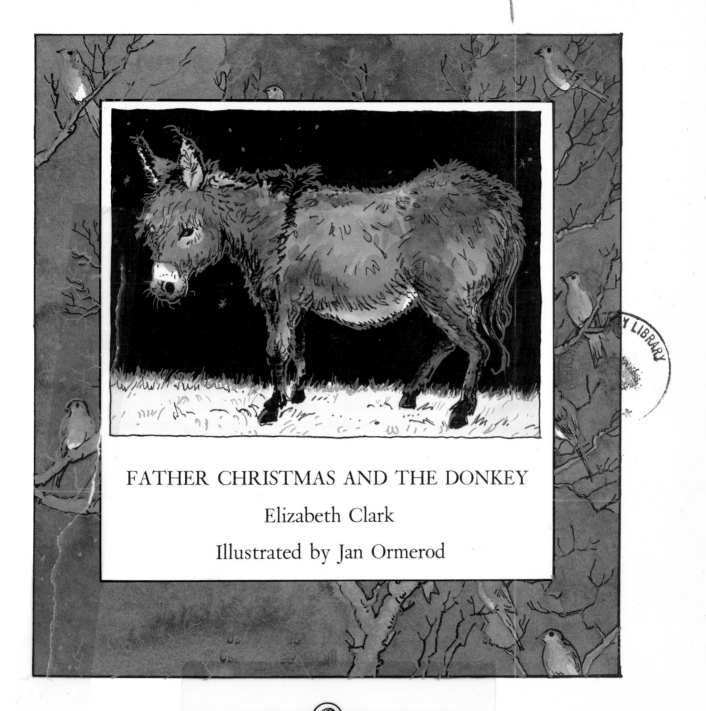

FATHER CHRISTMAS AND THE DONKEY

Elizabeth Clark

Illustrated by Jan Ormerod

It was Christmas Eve and the night was very quiet and still. The stars and the little moon sparkled in the sky and the frost sparkled on the grass. It was a clear night, but it was very cold.
The old shaggy donkey who lived on the common was limping

"Warm straw and hay," he said to himself, "warm straw and hay." The thought made him feel hungry, and he put his nose down and snuffled and blew among the grass tufts to find something to eat. But the grass was all stiff and frosted. It tickled his nose and made him sneeze and sneeze. "Broo-oo-oof," said the donkey. He shook his head hard till his ears flapped, and brayed a long, mournful bray. "Eee-aw-ee-aw-ee-aw-ee-aw-aw-aw-aw!" The donkey stood there with his neck stretched out and his ears laid back and his tail tucked in between his legs — a sad, shaggy, lame old donkey.

Down in the valley the church clock began to strike twelve. Each stroke sounded loud and clear in the stillness. As the clock finished striking, there came another sound. The donkey pricked up his ears and listened.

There was a little shivery, silvery tinkling in the air, a tiny, far-off sound as if the stars above were tingling. It came nearer and nearer still. Then it seemed to the donkey that somewhere overhead something went rushing by with a clear, sweet ringing like silver bells and a noise of far-away hoofs galloping fast.

It was an exciting kind of noise. It made the donkey feel as if he must gallop too. He could not remember galloping since he was a baby donkey with his mother. He tucked in his head and his ears and his tail as donkeys do when they gallop, and he was just going to try – in spite of his lame leg – when he heard another sound. Somebody was coming up the hill.

The donkey waited and listened. He could hear footsteps crunching a little on the frosty grass. Then he saw somebody coming towards him – somebody tall and big in a long, shaggy, white fur coat with a white fur hood pulled up over his head and big, fur-topped boots on his feet. As he came nearer, the donkey could see that he had a long, white beard, and under his white fur hood his eyes shone and twinkled like two bright stars. There was a large sack upon his shoulders. It was tied in the middle, but both ends bulged and hung down as if it was full of interesting things of all shapes and sizes. He was puffing a little, as if the sack was heavy to carry up the hill. His breath was like a little cloud in the frosty air. He looked at the donkey and the donkey looked at him.

The donkey was feeling still more excited. He was happy too, not grumpy any more. There seemed to be a wonderful, kind, warm, friendly feeling all around. And then a very kind voice said, "Happy Christmas, friend donkey. I heard you calling and you sounded lonely, so I came."

"I was lonely," said the donkey, "and I'm glad you came. Excuse my asking, but would you mind telling me who you are?"

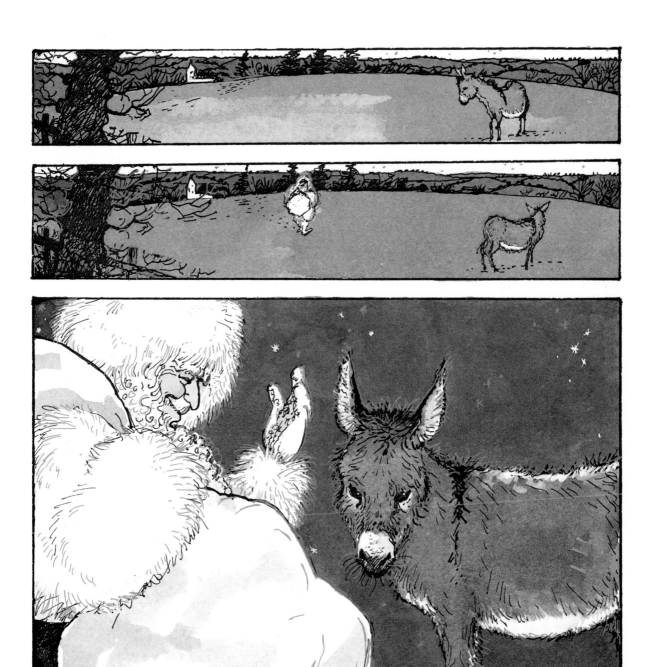

And the friendly voice said, "Some people call me Father Christmas and some say Santa Claus. It's all the same really."

"I remember now," said the donkey, "the brown cow told me about you. But she said that you came in a sledge with reindeer," said the donkey in a puzzled voice.

"So I do," said Father Christmas, "so I do. But I've sent them home tonight. It's after twelve o'clock. Didn't you hear the sledge-bells go by?"

"Oh-h-h!" said the donkey. "So that was it."

"Yes," said Father Christmas, "that was it. They've been a long, long way tonight. Here, there and everywhere we've been, all over the world – north, south, east and west – finding the children. Children from France, children from Germany, children from America and children from Australia, children from Norway and Russia and Africa and ever so many other places. Wherever they are, we've found them."

"So when twelve o'clock struck," said Father Christmas, " 'Home!' I said to the reindeer. There's only this sackful to take to Green Lane Hollow and a few places on the way. I can carry that myself."

The donkey looked at the sack. It was large and it was bulgy and it was certainly heavy. "Green Lane Hollow is twelve miles away," he said.

Father Christmas smiled at him. "If I keep on walking," he said, "I shall get there."

"Couldn't I help?" said the donkey. "I could carry the sack."

"Why," said Father Christmas, "so you could." He looked at the donkey very affectionately. "But what about your leg?"

"I can manage," said the donkey stoutly.

"So you shall," said Father Christmas. "So you shall."

He laid the sack across the donkey's back and they set out. Across the common they went and down a narrow lane, then up a steep hill and along the high road.

On and on they journeyed. The sack was heavy, but the donkey's back was strong, and though his leg was stiff, it was wonderful how little it hurt.

On and on they went. Sometimes the road dipped into hollows where it was dark. Then Father Christmas went ahead, to show the way. There was a kind of shining round him and it was quite easy to follow him.

But mostly Father Christmas walked beside the donkey with his hand resting on the donkey's shoulders, just where the dark cross-mark showed on the shaggy, mouse-coloured coat. It gave the donkey a wonderful, happy kind of warm glow to feel it there.

Every now and again, they stopped to leave a packet or a bundle by the door of a house or cottage. The donkey could feel that the sack was getting lighter. But there was still a good deal left in it when they came to the top of the long lane that led down to Green Lane Hollow.

Father Christmas looked up at the sky and nodded. "It's not long now till daylight," he said.

It was certainly a long lane. The stars were beginning to look pale and silvery, and there was a pinky look in the sky before they came to the bottom of the hill and saw a long, white cottage with a thatched roof. There were comfortable little noises of hens clucking and waking and a cow lowing in a shed.

The house looked fast asleep. All the windows were dark and all the curtains were drawn. But as the donkey and Father Christmas came down the lane, they saw a little chink of light in a window and smoke began to fluff out of a chimney.

"That's old Mrs Honeywell," said Father Christmas. "She's stirring up the fire. The house will be wide awake in a moment. It's time for me to be going."

"Happy Christmas," said Father Christmas softly to the donkey. He stooped and kissed him on his velvety nose. His beard was warm and tickly and soft. The donkey wanted to sneeze – but the sneeze turned into a bray – a most tremendous bray.

"Ee-aw-ee-aw-ee-aw," said the donkey. He heard someone give a little chuckle and he felt something touch his ears. He looked about, but Father Christmas was gone.

But the cottage was awake – wide awake. The door flew open and there stood old Mrs Honeywell. The curtains rustled back and the windows creaked up and there was Mr Honeywell, leaning out of one window, and two children at the window beyond. They were all staring at the donkey. And who wouldn't stare if they looked out of their window on Christmas Day and saw a donkey standing there, with a sack upon his back?

"Bless me!" said Mrs Honeywell. "Where did he come from? And he's got a note pinned on his head!" Hanging from the donkey's ears was a neat little label. It said: "I bring Happy Christmas to Green Lane Hollow."

Mrs Honeywell patted the donkey and gave him an apple to eat. Then she turned the sack out on the kitchen floor.

There was a football and four red jerseys for the boys. There was a blue, woollen coat for Mrs Honeywell, and a knitted waistcoat for Mr Honeywell. There was a plum pudding in a basin and a bottle of sweets. No wonder the sack had felt bumpy!

But the boys seemed to think that the donkey was the best Christmas present of all. They patted him and petted him. Mrs Honeywell gave him another apple and Mr Honeywell gave him an armful of hay. Everyone was happy, but the donkey was happiest of all.

That was Christmas Day, and the donkey has been at Green Lane
Hollow ever since. He has grown quite sleek. The boys have
brushed and combed his coat, Mr Honeywell has treated his lame
leg, and sometimes the donkey pulls a little cart that is never too

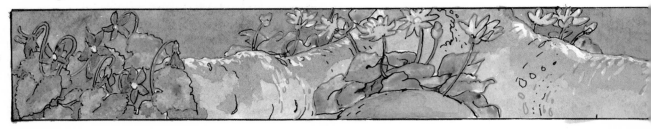

heavily loaded and trots along the road to the village when Mrs Honeywell goes shopping. In the summer he helps with the hay-harvest, and when the boys are not in school, one or other of them can be found on his back. He is a happy and contented old donkey.

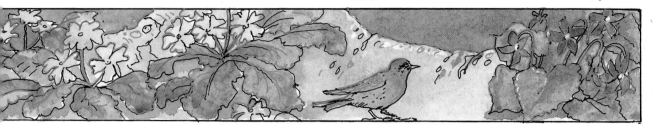

PUFFIN BOOKS

Published by the Penguin Group
Penguin Books Ltd, 27 Wrights Lane, London W8 5TZ, England
Penguin Books USA Inc., 375 Hudson Street, New York, New York 10014, USA
Penguin Books Australia Ltd, Ringwood, Victoria, Australia
Penguin Books Canada Ltd, 10 Alcorn Avenue, Toronto, Ontario, Canada M4V 3B2
Penguin Books (NZ) Ltd, 182–190 Wairau Road, Auckland 10, New Zealand

Penguin Books Ltd, Registered Offices: Harmondsworth, Middlesex, England

First published by Viking 1993
Published in Puffin Books 1995
1 3 5 7 9 10 8 6 4 2

Filmset in Monotype Van Dijck

PRINTED IN BELGIUM BY

INTERNATIONAL BOOK PRODUCTION